Originally published by
© 1979, Editions Duculot, Paris-Gembloux

Original title "Les Jouets Du Père Noël"

North American edition published under special license
Copyright © 1980, Annick Press, Toronto, Canada

Canadian Cataloguing in Publication Data

Passegand, Evelyne.
Santa's own toys

Translation of Les jouets du Père Noël.

ISBN 0-920236-12-X

I. Sacré, Marie-José. II. Title.

PZ7.P38Sa   j843.914   C80-094000-8

Printed in Italy

SANTA'S OWN TOYS

Text • Evelyne Passegand
Illustrations • Marie-José Sacré

Annick Press
Toronto, Canada

Once upon a time, long ago, Santa Claus got into a lot of
trouble. He was a man with a big white beard, but he was
not old. Sometimes he was a little silly. He loved doing
somersaults, sliding on frozen ponds, tobogganing and
eating candy. Grown-ups bored him, especially parents.
"They're dull," he used to say. "They never swing their
legs when they sit on chairs, or chew bubble gum, or draw
on frozen windows with their fingers."
"Stop grumbling," his mother would say, "and take that
candy out of your mouth."
Santa Claus tried to hide his candy by moving it from one
cheek to the other. Then he took out his chewing gum and
stuck it in his beard, so that he could have another chew
later.

One day Santa Claus had already eaten two chocolate
bars, a box of candied fruit and a whole handful of toffees.
He had made a ball of chewing gum almost too big to fit
into his mouth. Now he was in the middle of sucking on
five lollipops because he was bored.
"I wonder what the children are doing," he said to his
mother.

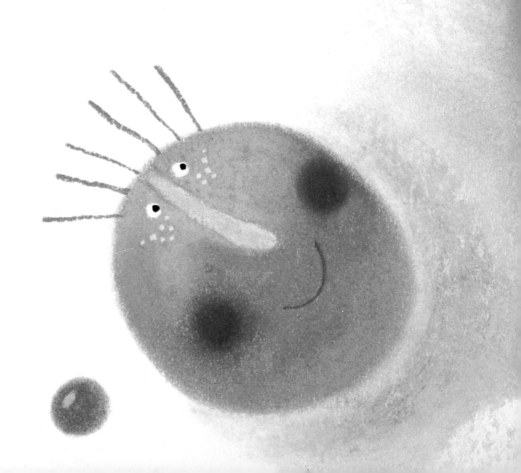

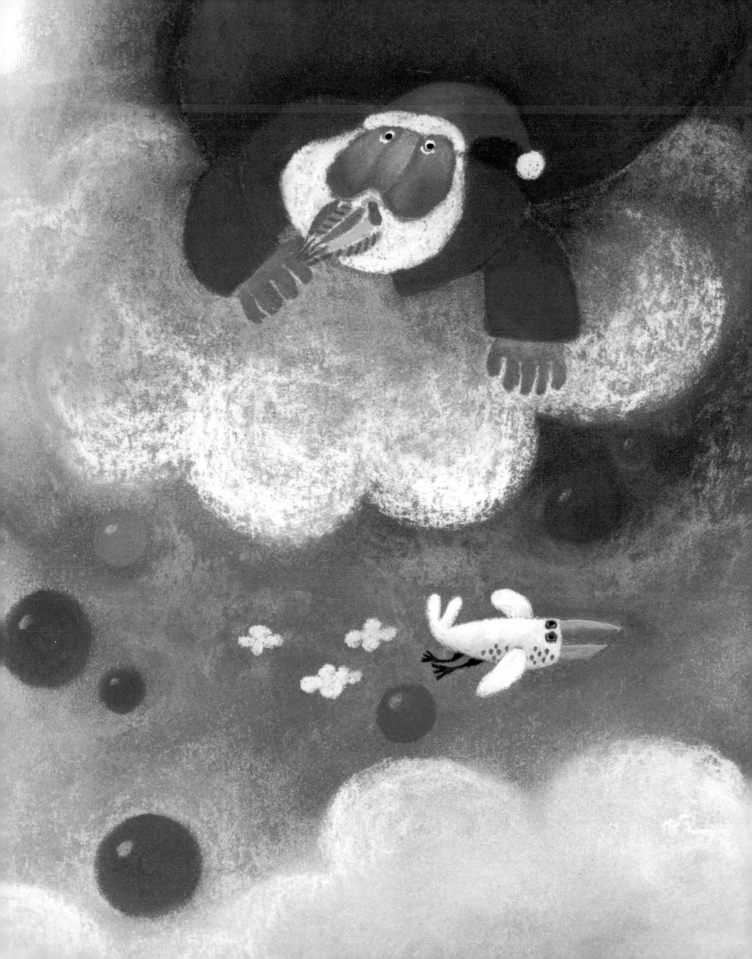

"Why don't you make some toys for the children," she said. "That'll keep you busy. Those candies will ruin your teeth. You are bothering me, sitting there with your snowball melting all over the floor."

"Me *make* toys? For children? You must be crazy," said Santa Claus. "What a funny idea. I don't *make* them, I *bring* them."

"But you could make much better toys than they have in the stores, toys with which the children could pretend," said his mother. "When children play, they like to *pretend*. How can you *pretend* a thing is a horse, when it already *looks* like a horse."

Santa Claus thought and thought. Then, starting with 18 pieces of bubble gum, he invented toys that were truly different. First he made things that were round like the bubbles he had blown.

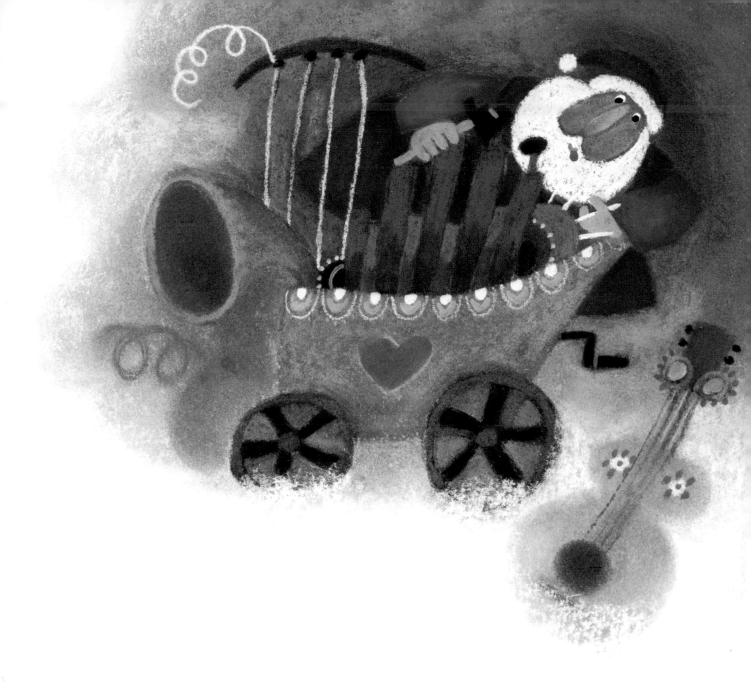

He made toys that sounded like the wind in the trees or
far-away music. He made toys as slippery as ice, as
boisterous as storms, as changeable as dreams. He made
colours that you could smell and tastes you could touch
and sounds you could break into pieces and put together
again. His toys were quite different from all the others.

That was the most magnificent
Christmas children had ever known.
Under each Christmas tree were two
piles of presents. On one side were the
toys that the parents has bought. On
the other were the extraordinary
surprises made by Santa Claus, toys
that sang with light and floated in
colour.
The children paid little attention to the
parents' presents.

The parents were quite upset, of course. They wrote nasty letters to Santa Claus, saying, "Don't ever come back! We don't need your help! Goodbye."

When he read these letters Santa Claus became very angry. His face went bright red. He threw a snowball so hard at a nearby star, he almost put it out.

His mother was so scared that she dived under her snowflake eiderdown and stayed there all day.

"Okay," said Santa Claus when he had finished reading all the letters. "If that's how they feel, they can do the job themselves. Why should I bother?"

When Christmas came around again, the children found
nothing from Santa Claus. They searched everywhere for
his toys, in their beds, under the carpets, in the closets
and drawers, even inside books. Not one, anywhere.
There were the usual presents from their parents in the
usual place beside the Christmas tree, but nothing else.
They thanked their parents for their gifts, but inside, they
sadly thought, "Santa Claus isn't coming any more."

Only one girl made a drawing to explain to Santa Claus
how much the children had liked his presents. She
wrapped it in a tight little package with a piece of cake
and, pointing out the right direction, she asked a bird to
take it to him at the North Pole.
And the following Christmas he came back.

At the foot of each Christmas tree he found a parent
arranging presents. "What are *you* doing here?" they said
to him. "Get out of here."
Santa Claus just thumbed his nose at them. "Now off you
go," said one mother, "or you'll make me angry."
Santa Claus stuck out his tongue.

The mother said, "Look! We want our children to play with the toys that *we buy* for them."
Santa Claus took out of his sack a whispering breeze you could hold, candies that sang as you ate them, a mist that bounced like a ball and shone, colours you could see through and talk into shapes. "What about these?" he said.
The mother angrily picked up his wonderful toys and threw them after Santa Claus who was running out the door.

All that remained were broken pieces. The children later picked them up and looked at them. "Not very exciting," they said. "It must be some new kind of building blocks. Funny." But they played with them for a long time. And they sadly thought, "Santa Claus isn't coming any more."

So Santa Claus returned home. One of the toys thrown after him had hit him on the thumb. His mother put a big bandage on it and said, "If they don't believe you'll come, you'd better stay home next year."

But Santa Claus was stubborn. He pushed his candy from one cheek to the other and thought, "If I made presents the grown-ups can't see, maybe then it would be alright. If I slide down the chimneys at night, when everybody is asleep, they'll never know. But the children will know I was there."

Since that day a peculiar thing has puzzled grown-ups every year. Sometimes the children talk to and play with things that aren't really there, or at least, things that can't be seen. Parents may say, "I wonder what the children are up to?" But the children know what they are doing. They are playing with Santa's gifts.